Their name had three letters...

THREE

LETTER

LOVERS

A Poetic Journal of Youthful Infatuation, Heartbreak and Silence

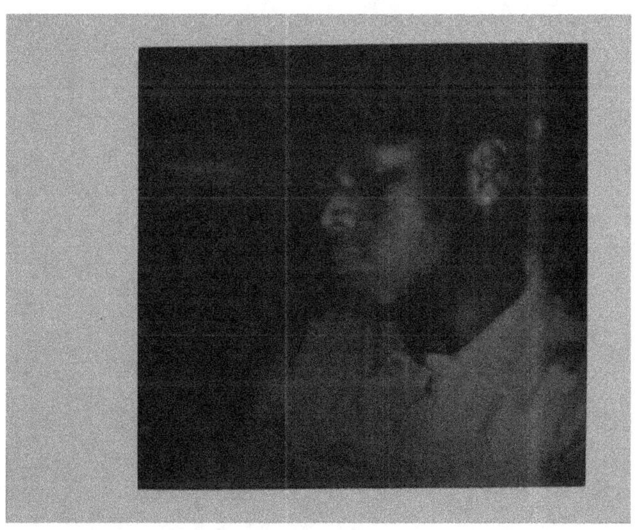

www.gabekanae.com

First Edition

ISBN: 979-8-9869717-0-4 (paperback)

ISBN: 979-8-9869717-1-1 (hardback)

ISBN: 979-8-9869717-2-8 (ebook)

Library of Congress Control Number: 2022917575

A Book by Gabe Kanae

TABLE OF CONTENTS

(Tracklist)

I

II

III

IV

I've never been one to say goodbye easily and I've never been one to say goodbye at all, so, this book is filled with a lot of dread. It wasn't my direct intention, but I constantly kept writing these pages to encapsulate the deep and masked thoughts that sometimes exist. These pages are a diverse collection of song lyrics I have written over the years, fictional thoughts and non-fictional thoughts I have finally, courageously, decided to share.

That said, the majority of this book takes place in 2021. The most intense and surreal year of my life so far. It was filled with so much greatness, love and friendship. It was also countered by heartbreak, self-loathing, invalidation, and abuse of my love and worth.

Not knowing what is real or fake in this book is the most intriguing part of it for me and I hope it will be to you as well. This is my first ever piece of writing outside of journalism that I have published, and I have also taken into account that a lot of the readers are people who solely caused some of these pages to exist how they do, whether good or bad.

I wanted this to be the first introduction to my writing (though I am working on other visual and textual projects) because each page elicits and provokes a different emotion, thought, reality and realization. I just hope you will see that within these pages is the vulnerability and the emotional weight I carried at eighteen and in my first semester of college.

I want to thank anyone who actually bought this book, whether because they felt intrigued or because I had told them of its existence. I appreciate you so much.

When it comes to creativity, one of the craziest things I've learned by observation of artists, is that there is literally no right. No matter who makes what or how, nothing can please everyone. It truly is one of the worst things about being a creator (in my opinion). As a creator and artist, it is hard to release something you're so specific about and want to be perfect because you've been taught only perfection can make you. Now, I try not to let perfection be a reason to hold me back. This book is an example of that.

I've learned that if I hold a product back and keep re-reading and editing … nothing will ever get completed. I am nervous of releasing this book and also seeing you read it and criticize it, how it effects your emotions or how upsetting it is to you. I just hope you can let me, as an artist, learn what happens.

You're about to read a poetry book written by an eighteen / nineteen-year-old teenager that is comprised of thoughts, experiences, journal entries and ideas from my present and past and how other people's actions have impacted them. I hope, if what you did as a person is talked about in this book, you will have an open mind. Many of the emotions on these pages have changed. Some have stayed the same. Some aren't even real.

I hope you enjoy my first book. I hope it intrigues and potentially ends up earning a space on your bookshelf at home. I hope my experiences can open your mind to the world and how diverse it is. I hope you can respect it, me, and the vulnerability and mistakes that each letter may or may not create.

G.K.

Dedicated To

My Family,

Toby,

everyone who helped me survive to write these pages,

including
me.

All images are shot on 35mm or instant film.

I remember your arms...
and when I do it just adds more tears
that dry on the pages of my journal.
Forever wrinkled.

You said you loved me,
why'd you leave?
Did you think it wouldn't hurt?

You were the first person I met since
I was bullied out of high school.
You were my first friend since
the quarantine.
You were the first person who cared about me.
Really.
I meant it when I said you were all I needed.

Now my journal entries are wet,
ink blots as our memories rot,
stained by the pain you left.
I wish it was how it could've been.

The biggest trigger for my tears
are the words I've said for a year.
"I just miss my friend"
I can't say it without a breakdown.

You've never seen my eyes wet.
It has happened so much since you left.
I'll always have an opening in my heart for you.
One you could repair if you tried...
if you tried.

I remember our moments.
When I wasn't with you, knowing I was with you,
my three letter lover.
Now when I try and scan my journal,
I realize that you can't read it anymore.
Dry wrinkles smudging the words.
Now I have to transcribe it on a computer page.
As I type, I'll cry.

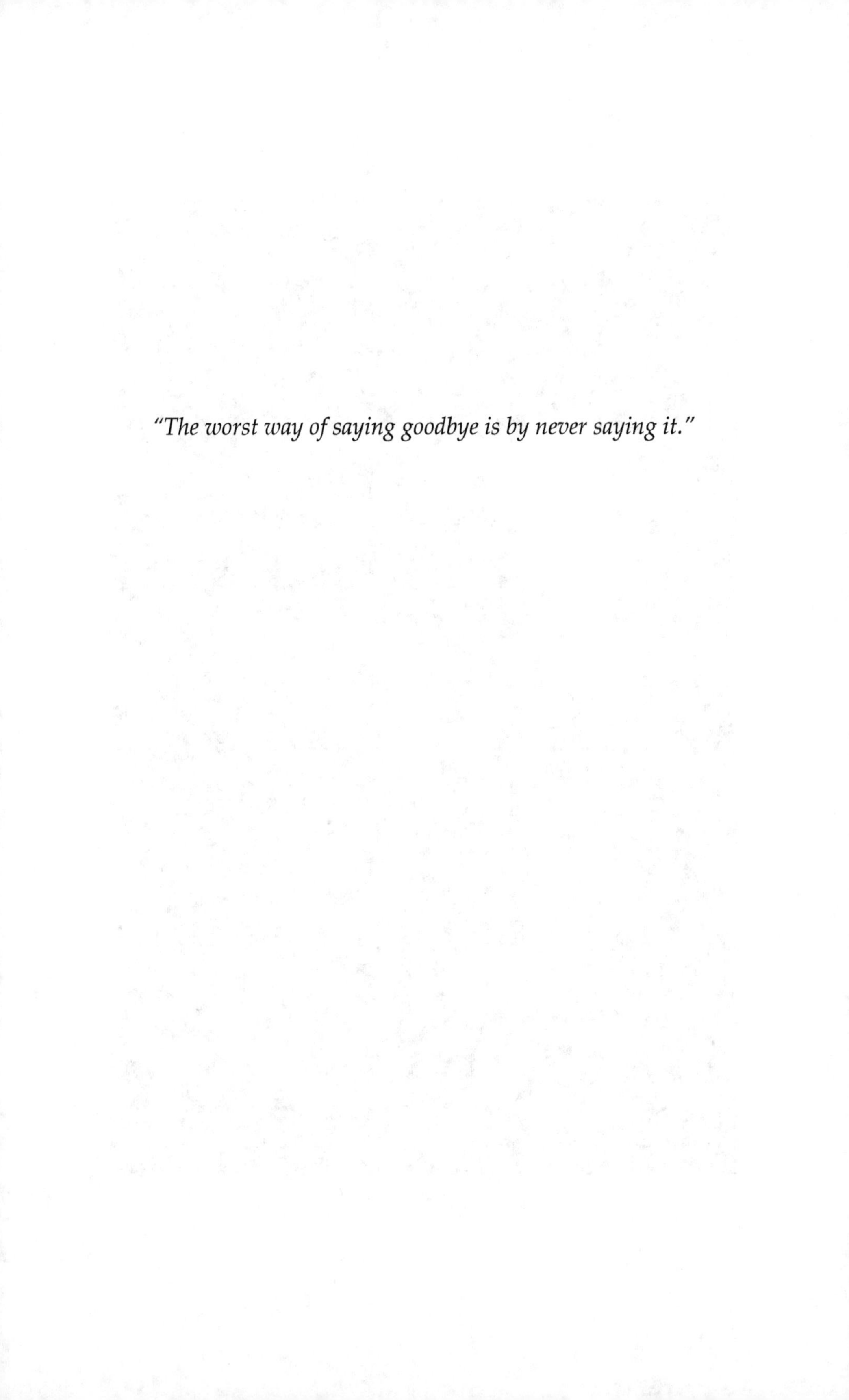
"The worst way of saying goodbye is by never saying it."

<u>I</u>

Passion and Pain

UNKNOWN DIRECTION
G.K.

Within summer heat,
where the heat waves simmer,
one remains.

Unknown of how,
proper or improper,
they remain.

Quivering quails,
fierce horror,
they cry.

Written microphone,
amplified,
they write.

GONE BUT LOVED

G.K.

Loving
Cuddling,
    both of them were.

Lonely
Hoping,
    losing their tropes.

Physically
Mentally,
    emotionally not there.

Sight
Lost,
    nothing will compare.

Complexion,
    beyond anything thought.

Despicable
Riddled,
    gone they were.

I'VE NEVER
G.K.

I've never watched somebody like I watched you.
Spent my nights laughing in your June,
I still remember the scent of your perfume as your fingers
twisted in my curls.
I never knew heartbreak could get this worse.

I still look back to the night right before.
There's no point of working if we're not working it out.
Our fight leaving the deepest cuts.
Shattering memories, a dead dove.
Our fine medial lust.

I miss your clues and your brightest smile.
The swift movements that made me wild.
Keeping your contact on speed-dial.
Your unbroken state of nature and how you ran a mile.
How your hourglass body was perfect for any style.

I wish I wasn't that vile.
I wish I could take back the offhanded comments that broke
our survival.
I'd take it all back, I'm tired of this spiral.

* * *

I also wish you kept the promises you said you'd keep.
Instead, I woke up in the morning to news,
it made me weep.
You took your gun and I could've saved you if I were across
the street.
I wish you could've come to me.

Your broken heart was pulled by the other guy.
Your family built broken, filled with so much emotion.
I can't fix what's gone.
I never knew heartbreak could get this worse.

I wish my mind didn't make me pile all that shit onto you so
maybe we would've stayed together.
I can't touch the things you once touched.
They hold the memory that was between us.
I wish I could take you in for that hug.
The one I promised I'd give when we pushed through the fire.
We never did.
I never did.
I never knew heartbreak could get this worse.

FELLOW

G.K.

what was thought
is no longer there

the things we bought
now bring despair

simple answers
to end a drought

many questions
bringing many thoughts

glistening eyes
shined by tears

hopefully we'll forget this
in a couple years

...

FORWARD
G.K.

Forward.
Forward.
You may
>   push.
Forward.
Forward.
For you to
>   forever
>   regret.
Forward.
Forward.
You may seem
>   but there are things,
>   many indeed.
Forward.
Froward.
Your genetic
>   luck.
Forward.
Forward.
>   nepotism must
>   really suck.
Forward.

Forward.
	you'll plant a tree.
Forward.
Forward.
	no diversity,
	there will be.
Foreword.
Foreword.
	I will,
	always be.

BARE

G.K.

Bare

Babe

Bane

Pain

Pair

Plant

Sort

Simply

Secondly

There

Their

They're

Love

Lair

Liar

Fair

Care

Rare

Confront

Confuse

Compile

Comply

* * *

something only a combination of words
can buy.

DORM
G.K.

Blue eyes,
Our careful love ties,
It might've all just been a lie.

Regrets,
your silhouette,

I miss when your love was mine.

My dorm faces your place,
I sometimes see your face,
and you've seen mine,

I think you forgot about my blue butterfly,
it never forgot about you…
oh I fucking miss you

My blue butterfly
flies by the ocean side
something you loved
I guess I just wasn't enough

CLOSE TO YOU

G.K.

You gave reason to the stares.

Happiness from the glares.

I hate when you'd cry in your room.

But you never cared about my heart,
and how badly I fell for you.

I gave you the hope, that reassurance,
just to help you feel so cool.

Now you're in your room,
wishing I was,

still close to you

PROJECT

G.K.

Project,
after
Project.

Skip to the next.

Project,
after
Project.

Constant regret.

Project,
after
Project.

Pencil unsharpened.

Project,
after
Project.

I project on these pages.

EYES

G.K.

Why is it that eyes can tell such a story?
What is at home,
or even a reaction to a story.

Eyes can love.
Eyes can die.
Eyes keep the picture
in your eye.

Concentration,
representation,
eyes can be the unique
signs of you

Whether,
lake waves,
brown forests,
yellow sap
and
green leaves

an eye can tell a lie
that can easily deceive.

BASIN
G.K.

Basin tales
ring and ring.
From drunk night sleeps
to homework weeps.

Many say the Basin is great,
while others would say different about
Room 508.

Twin XL,
cranking at night,
a rush of a job,
That sometimes creates life.

Variety,
prevail,
geeky,
it may seem,

but,

there's always something interesting
occurring every week.

* * *

Great Basin's alarm can beep,
it just shows the safety we seek.
The doors lock, some with a key,

and the only thing that matters
is…
the people you meet.

NEW CONTINUATION
G.K.

New contact,
he didn't know I heard.
I wish to give contact,
but it will only lead to hurt

A fix is all I want,
it's easy to conceive.

A fix is all I want,
but it's something
I won't receive.

SEAGULL
G.K.

Flocking the sky,
cloud by cloud,

a simple birds eye, more
than enough to spy

How can seagull mean so well,
when its white feathers blend in,
so well.

Ambitious, unique, special,
never ill

A seagull has so much power
I won't ever feel.

ASH
G.K.

Ash rains down.
It reminds me of the very first day.

Grand cute eyes
Blonde, wavy hair.

       It must've felt easy to be in so much control,
          of people's lives and how it goes.

Detail enriched,
A drought will soon come…

And nearly instantly,

       Clear skies appear
       as Ash disappears.
      All this for manipulative little Ash.

NEWS
G.K.

There's experience with the news.
Something I really did not expect.

A new job,
perhaps a new story to tell

Though during the call of initiation,
it was so quite scary.

Like a mini-interview,
a quiet judgment,
even though it is unknown.

I am quite scared,
hearing about the job.
I wonder if I won't fit this job where I am,
in my mental hill.

CRASH COURSE
G.K.

Crash course of what we had.
Evil tears,
formed from a sinister past.

Crash course of the love we built.
The nailed in pieces that protected us
and made us last.

Courses are always hard to understand,
but it is even harder to accept
when you're picking up the pieces from the
crash.

Memory-stained walls,
that saw our dance.
Pieces of a bed frame,
that used to always last.

Sometimes I miss running through the halls,
hand in hand.
Lips on lips.
Laugh to laugh.

Sometimes I miss you,

what we had.
How a sinister past,
is why we didn't last.

DROUGHT
G.K.

Every day it seems the drought never ends.
I'll feel a form of moisture, but it never lasts.
I sabotage myself into wanting more than I can.
Forcing myself to work, and when I don't, it's bad.
I wonder how this was founded. Likely from the fast.
Maybe I waited too long.
Maybe I just am beginning.
Maybe right now, I am not who I think I am.
Potentially better, but why can't I see?
I see a shadow, but the sun just makes it disappear. I
rethink, over-complicate, everything I say.
Everything I make isn't a good thing.
It's just a mistake.

When will this ever feel right.
When will I actually gain my worth?
I've tried to work on it,
but it never works.
Every day turns to a night
and every day I upset myself,
because of my might.
Exhaustion, depression, staying inside,
I just want to be successful.

Something others look at to have pride.

Or maybe they already do.
Or is it selfish to think so brightly of myself?
Who?

CRYSTAL
G.K.

Sparking,
no pattern.
Blue blimps.
Flash and flash again.

It's a mental state.
Constant rate.
Always taking the bait.

Sandstone,
growing.
A miner,
bringing it back to the gates.
So, he can eat.
And he ate.

His family is new.
His children are great.
His wife left him.
She couldn't handle the hate.

He's a bad man,
does he deserve to have nothing?

CHANGE OF TIMES
G.K.

It's hard for me to feel how I did years ago. Before
I learned how cruel this world is.
How easy it is to ridicule and hate,
never seeing what it takes from another,
who is already bait.

It's hard to forget how unkind I've been treated.
Let alone treat others with such unforgiving takes.
How could I?
They just keep taking from my bank.

It's hard for me to convince myself to love myself,
when most people just want to hate me.
Why would I deserve to like myself
for the nit-picky mistakes?

This is the main reason I want to die.
To cure the world from another guy.
But I need to be here for some.
Not for me.

I haven't wanted me to be here since eighth grade.
That's what anonymous hate takes.

They don't have to take accountability for what they did.
Only I do.

Do I ever cross their minds?
Or did they forget what they take?
Change of times, out of mind.

STANDARD

G.K.

I will never fit the standard.
The standard may never fit me.
I'm not sure why patriarchy is so mean.
Particular, slim-fit and crude,
would leaving the internet help forget these rules?
Possessive,
progressive,
potential,
probable,
perfect,
quirky,
but mean,
what am I supposed to be?
Skinny? I wish.
Smart? That's a risk.
When I'm me, it doesn't feel right.
Too many eyes latch on,
making me no longer out of sight.
I don't know what I'm supposed to be.
It makes me upset not knowing what I need.

APPLICATION
G.K.

An application so intense and cruel.
So objectified, treating everyone like a tool.
All that to gain some satisfaction
From someone you don't even know
who doesn't even feel attraction.
Does anyone think about how it feels
to be so misunderstood?
To be easily forgotten and replaced
with a tap or reply action.

I'm not their type.
Too big or annoying indeed.
Maybe it's just because I offer love,
something they don't need.
Maybe they just want to have fun.
Maybe I'm just waiting for the one.

The one who'll understand me and why,
I gave him my love, something you can't buy.
I tried and I tried and now I must stop,
because every offer I give is not taken a lot.
When it is, after a few months,
it brings no appeal.

Just pain.

I need to learn how to feel.

But first, I need to learn how to heal.

M vs. M
G.K.

Majority
Vs.
Minority

You won the battle,
you were already on the hill.
How does it feel?

It's crazy that a majority tried to split friendships
from a minority because he was twelve feet closer
to sharing that hill.

It had to be you.
Only you.
You had reign because everything I did was not
enough.

You played rough.
Made you feel tough.

You won.
How does it feel?

FLASH
G.K.

Flash.
Flash.
Bash.

Flash.
Flash.
Mash.

Flash.
Flash.
You're not enough.

Flash.
Flash.
You're replaced,

         by another ace.

SPOT
G.K.

Does that spot hurt your heart?
The area of the mart,
where we laughed a lot.
I remember your heart,
I think you remember mine.
I miss carrying you in my arms
after midnight.

I visit that spot.
It's hard to see it there.
To see others in it,
not seeing what was there.

REPETITION
G.K.

You promise?
  Yes.
You swear?
  Yes.
Okay. Good. Let's move on.

You promise?
  Yes.
You swear?
  Yes.
Okay. Good. Let's move on.

You promise?
  Yes.
You swear?
  Yes.
Okay. Good. Let's move on.

You promise?
  Yes.
You swear?
  Yes.
Okay. Good. Let's move on.

You promise?
        Yes.
You swear?
        Yes.
Okay. Good. Let's move on.

EDWARD

G.K.

I don't hate many, but Edward is one I do.
Someone who ruins many people's lives.
Possibly even you.
Edward has caused nothing but pain. It's
easy to fall into his plans.
Crumble into his game.

How is it so easy to fall down the hole
but takes years to dig yourself out?
Why is the ride down faster,
then the grueling ride up?

Why does it take so long to forget
the good that was given?
Why does it take so long to forget
what was taken?
Why would you want to forget
life before Edward?

That's the hardest part, trying to break free of his game.

IN MY BED AT NOON
G.K.

In my bed at noon,
no sleep at night.
I've got an off-sleep schedule,
just watching the world pass around me,
as I exist but only partly.

That's the wild.
I'm in the wild.
There's a mental wild,
that goes wild,
staying inside.

I used to hate staying inside.
Now, sometimes it is nice to stay inside,
at least, I think.
Sometimes it is nice to stay inside,
sometimes.

Sometimes I feel staying inside,
is where I can be my best side.
Letting creativity exist,
me and my plants.

* * *

Sometimes it is nice to stay inside,
at least, I think.
Sometimes it is nice to stay inside,
sometimes.

FAKE YOU
G.K.

Sometimes I do miss the fake you, Sarah.
The expressive and perfect you, Sarah.
The Sarah who cuddled and cared,
the Sarah I could kiss and love.

Sometimes I miss the old you, Sam.
When things felt normal, and I felt loved.
I miss when you cared for me, Sam.
I miss my boyfriend and friend, Sam.

Sarah, what I would do to hold you.
Feel your soft skin once again.
Forgetting about the bad in you Sarah.
Just to love you again Sarah.

Sam, what I would do to have the old you back.
The one who never questioned me.
The one that loved me for who I am.
I just want to love you, old Sam.

CREEK
G.K.

There's a creek,
where love is often made.
Rarely - do hearts break there,
that's where we met.

There's a swamp,
where love is often destroyed.
Rarely - do hearts love there,
that's where we broke.

There's a building,
where mixes of love are expressed.
Love is just not talked about there,
that's where I am after you left.

There's a place,
where our love can meet.
Love can come back there,
but you continue to run.

There's a girl.
A girl I loved.
Her blonde hair brushing on her shoulder.

I miss her love.
Now, she's with someone.

YOUTHFUL

G.K.

I used to be youthful,
I used to be innocent,
I used to be strong.

Something took it from me.
Something stole that from me.
Something pushed that away from me.

I'm not yet sure what fully remains.
I'm not yet sure what maturity is like,
I'm not yet sure what I do with it.

THREE LETTER LOVERS

G.K.

Do you remember me?
What we used to be?

Texted at midnight,
had Snapchat streaks,
was in love with me

Three letter lovers are mean.
Break your heart into threes,
why do you mean so much to me?
We only lasted three weeks.

Three letter lovers,
staying as long as their name
but gives you so much pain.

WESTERN TO MODERN
G.K.

Western to modern.
Something the ground under our feet know
too well.

It's so easily to forget,
and disrespect
things that have always been here.

The sky,
many of the stars,
the ground that horses once ran on,
cowboy by its side.

Western to modern.
Legacy to nothing.

We might be the new western.
Forgotten by another modern.
But, never let your horse forget you,
it's one of those things that make the western matter.

TAP
G.K.

I tap into my brain.
It's a wild mess.
It's built off of others,
and all of their offense
at me.

Tip tap into every situation.
I somehow am always wrong.
Maybe going away,
will solve others pain
from me?

I don't know how
it would all go down.
When, or, how.
I don't want it to go south,
hope it ends me.

NOTEPAD

G.K.

I hate that my notepad tells me what I should think.
How I should feel,
how I should move.

I hate that my diary is a gateway to my pain.
How it felt,
how it feels.

I hate that my mind works the way it works.
Broken and bent,
broken and ruined.

PLANT GREEN
G.K.

Plant green.
So beautiful type of green.

Plant green.
Adopted and grown,
lies on my windowsill.

Plant green,
loved and watered,
wealthy and healthy,
given a name.

Plant green.
Always so pretty,
always adapting,
always watching,
always learning.

Plant green,
so pretty.

CUT

G.K.

Cutting ties is hard.
It's hard to mourn someone
who is still alive.

Cutting ties is hard.
It's hard to care for someone
who left you to die.

Cutting ties is hard.
It's hard to die for someone
who was never by your side.

BLUE SKIES

G.K.

The sky is blue,
not much rain.

The sky is blue,
me and my friends are celebrating
that moment of happiness we share.

I love my friends.
I love their kindness.
Their smile.
Their dedication.

The sky is blue.
It's easy to forget.
The weather may be hot, but at least,
The sky is blue, and,
my smile is white.

DECK
G.K.

Of course, it's the deck.

Not that there's wrong with the deck.
Not that there's bad with the deck.
It's just the good things with the deck for you
aren't the best about the deck for me.

Of course, it's the deck.

Where the wood splits,
and I almost fell that one time.
You don't remember that, how I do though.
Not how I did.

Of course, it's the deck.

And I'll still come anyway.

HATE. CLOUD.
G.K.

"What language is she speaking?"
"It's really getting out of hand"
"This shit is getting a bit carried away"
"How many genders do y'all have damn"
"I wouldn't be surprised if it has a penis"
"There's only 2 genders sorry to break it to you"

They go out of their way to deny someone's existence.
For what reason?
To never change?
To stay the same and never have any uniqueness.

There is already too much pain.
Too much anger. Too much hate.
Made by people like you.

How can we heal when we can never be accepted?

TWO MONTHS
G.K.

Two months since it got that bad.
A coping mechanism that's so sad.
I need to stay sober.
Be okay.
What will that take?
How can I be okay?

II
Writing Words

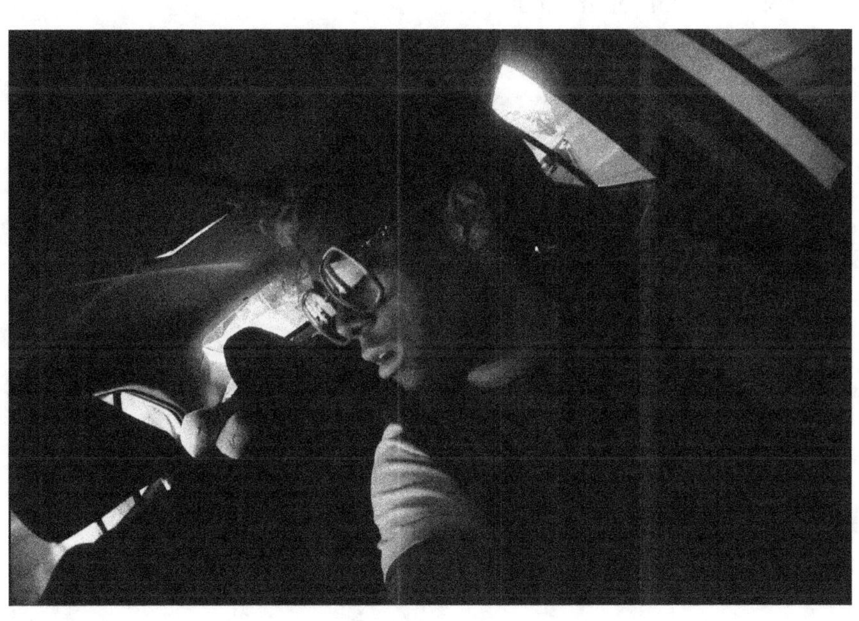

THE ART OF PROBLEM

G.K.

The art of problem is never-ending.
One thing to the next.
Problems can be valid.
Problems can be intense.
Problems can be never-ending.

The art of problem is the effect.
An effect that can never leave.
Effects have consequences.
If one will hold another accountable.

But they typically don't.
At least until the downhill ramp has started.
Neglecting the people hurt at the peak.

INDUSTRY MINDSET SWAP

G.K.

Swip swap,
gone and replaced.
Stability should remain,
but it never remains.

Swip swap,
come and gone.
Another life in debt.
Left for scraps.

Swip swap,
everyone thinks those who made it are rich.
But the riches take the riches,
and the artist gets nothing sweet.

NO WIN, STOP FIGHT
G.K.

Argumentation fights
end with a funny joke.
They think they won
but really, I'm just done.

There's no win.
No convincing.
No change of perceiving.

Stuck in their mind.
Stuck in their ways.
Nothing will change.
Nobody will take the blame.

No win, stop and fight,
bruise after bruise,
rarely is there light.

SCALE OF COMMENT

G.K.

It's easy to forget that
your comment was one
on top of hundreds of others
that combine and blur.

Each opinion,
each thought,
each comment,
all the same.
They contribute to the creator's mindset,
and who they think they are.

FEAR OF QUEER
G.K.

We live in a time
where acceptance is given to some
not to all however,
only few.

I hate that I have to be afraid of the impacts of picking
"Other" as my gender.

I hate that saying I'm not strictly a man is enough for people
to think of me badly.

I hate that also going by "they" is a reason to disrespect me.

If some can understand that sexuality is real, why can't
gender?

I wish we lived in a time
where acceptance was given to all.
Those who are against,
would leave us alone.

SOMETHING DIDN'T FEEL RIGHT
G.K.

Something didn't feel right
the last day.
You said it otherwise.

Something didn't feel right
when the dark cloud closed.
You said you couldn't see it.

Something didn't feel right.
I knew it all along…

THE TREE

G.K.

Pushed against a tree
was two people.
You and me,
holding hands and making permanent memories.

Now it's a decade later.
We're no longer part.
I'm with someone else.
They have my heart.
Not you.

You lay in the hotel bed,
awake
and
scared to return to work.
But your vacation just started,
so give each day it's worth.

You get out of bed,
hop in the rental car,
drive around your childhood town
and checked on the tree that's still around.

* * *

A tear falls from your crystal eye,
the one I said I loved
as we looked at the trail.

You've avoided who and where I am.
You continue too today.
Deep down I might still miss you.
Only now did you realize my love was rare.

FOR WHAT
G.K.

now I sit under a tree,

thinking all of this…

for love

tore my ankles till they bled,

cried under the doves,

questioned if

you're all okay with all this…

for none

I got all this pain

for what?

You dance at the party,

I've cried in the desert sitting

in the back of a bus.

Fire blazing high,

higher than we could be,

if only we could be.

* * *

all of this for what?

all of this for love?

I can't say it was fun.

MAYOR
G.K.

Mayor had to bail.
Some gay guy in his class loved his hair.
He ran and ran.
To no prevail.

COFFEE MAN
G.K.

Coffee man gentle,
his actions pronounced.
Kind and sweet,
hair brushed and soft.

His voice is one I'd love to have.
It gives a hug of care.
I wish I could be the coffee man,
but I don't even know what's in his lair.

His mind may be broken,
his family abused.
He may be perfect,
or maybe he's bruised.

I wonder if anyone ever wanted to be me.
Wanted to love me and see.
Has anyone ever wandered
and tried to love me as a dare?

NOWHERE BUT HERE
G.K.

I try to remind myself to be nowhere but here.
I just want to see the future
and if these words ever make it real.

Will I be able to live,
when everybody is gone?
Or am I going to hate myself
because I work a nine-to-five job?

This mindset isn't rare.
It's hard to bear.
But then,
I try to remind myself to be nowhere but here.

BEND WIND PEN

G.K.

My pen can write fast
but sometimes the paper is trash.
It ruins the whole product.
It makes it never last.

The bend can be missed.
A crash can occur.
You'd still drift the road,
never knowing what occurs.

The wind howls.
Everything feels sour.
Drive the trail.
Flatten the paper.
Let your hair blow in autumn air.

COFFEE AND WINE
G.K.

What does coffee and wine have in common?
Tastes are never the same in comparison.

What does coffee and wine actually have in common?
They help me work better and harder.

Coffee can help me breathe and work harder.
Wine can make me feel looser.

Coffee and wine are creative drinks.
Each with their own soul and foundation.
Just like art.

SUMMER AIR
G.K.

Driving down I-99,
windows rolled down,
letting in the summer air,
there could be nothing like it.
Your smile.
My eyes.
Pine needles flying in the car.
Ocean blue skies.

I drove down 99 the other day.
Saw the ghost of you and me.
A youthful capture.
That easily had in disguise
the toxicity and
the murder that
you had planned
for after the ride.
Your final goodbye.

GLASS SHOES

G.K.

Glass shoes can show regret,
if the one looking at it wears it and forgets.

Glass shoes,
Clean and new,
shiny and black,
nothing new.

There's nothing unique or special about these shoes,
until the one who sees it sees who's inside.
The bearer, the wearer,
the shoe's glistening in the sun.
The sharer, the care,
there aren't more than one.

RENO SOUP

G.K.

We had Reno soup right before you kissed my cheek.
We had Reno soup right after the Lake Tahoe ride.

You ghosted me, unfollowed me and thankfully you told me why.
It still hurt, but I'm grateful you did it the way you did.
It didn't make me want to die.

I saw you a few months later, hanging with your friends.
You were in the lobby of my dorm,
curly hair perfect, it was a ten.

I do kind of regret reaching out.
Being the reason, you blocked me,
being intrusive and unaccountable.

I hope you feel better.
I hope you smile.
I won't break any more boundaries;
I'll never get closer than a mile.

We had Reno soup, and you may have forgotten about it.
We had Reno soup and I'll never forget your smile.

HOW COULD YOU TWIST
G.K.

How could you *twist* that onto me?
Making me out to be the problem,
while you let it be.

You can't ignore mistakes you made.
How it can be understood,
and how you could be to blame.

How could you *twist* that onto me?
On a drive to the grave.
How could you *twist* that onto me?
When I was so smitten.

SO THAT IS WHY

G.K.

So that is why the silence was so loud.
Why the damp pieces of a puzzle can connect,
even by the smallest stem.
I'm not sure what I did.
It must've been the worst.
So that is why I'm still upset.

I told you I had anxiety.
I told you how to do this.
You promised.
What am I supposed to do when a promise made,
is one so simple, but also one you couldn't take?

I have never gotten an answer.
I have to look out into the horizon and fill in gaps,
I cannot.
It hurts more than most things I've felt.

I never told you why it meant so much. I will now.
You were the first person my age I had seen in years.
All we had was love.
My OCD riddled and controlled me.
It was hard for me to do anything.

When I was with you, I could do anything.
I could touch anything, there was no restriction.
I was able to open the door without a sleeve.
I was able to touch another without washing my hand.
When I was with you, OCD was gone.
Things were great.
Then they weren't.

When I realized,
I thought the silence was like the others.
I thought when I see you again, I would give you the biggest hug and cry deeply into your arms.
I thought that I was overreacting.
I anxiously thought it was actually over.
It was.
I never got to cry deeply into your arms.
Those tears hit my journal that in write in, every once in a while.
The ink is still smeared. Dried. Permanent.

I hope you get the quantities you desire.
You have yet to make my pain less dire.
One day, I hope you will.
So that is why it still hurts,
even though OCD can be gone without you now.

* * *

You took my innocence,
took who I was before,
took advantage of me being vulnerable,
naïve,
you made that wound so bloody it dripped for months while
you faced no consequence,
your friends will say you were right,
"he's weird",
what if they're wrong?
How many words do I need to write,
how many comments will it take,
for you to realize you need to be accountable for what you
did?

All I wanted was you.
All I took from you was time and love.
Maybe I hurt you.
I blame myself for that all of the time.
That's the biggest problem:
I don't know.

You knew not knowing would kill me.
It almost did.
I wrote these pages because it didn't.

Once, I drove down the freeway wondering what if.

Would you ever care enough to think?

What if the message from you is one you no longer could send?

TYPEWRITE
G.K.

Type.
Write.

What we might.

Type.
Write.

I miss every time I got to see a light.

Type.
Write.

I may fail, if I do, I hope I'll have mail.

SUPER SOLITUDE

G.K.

Photos of the Milky Way,
your eyes glistening as the fireworks blew,
the water under us crystal blue.
We knew,
it was like a movie scene;
unlike anything I've ever seen.
I wish I knew
that every single film good or bad,
has a climax.
When it did, we spew.
We knew it would end up like this.

Those things happened out there.
I hate to re-break your boundaries you set for me and you.
I hate to take you back to this place you left,
the feed affects me too.

My feed affects you.
Your feed affects me too.
We ran in the sand under the hot sun.
I thought I loved you once,
you said it was okay for me to gay.
After all that you left me in solitude.

Super solitude.

tude tude

Everything felt new without you.
You used to be my only friend. I
was lost in that mental place,
and you left me in
super solitude.

tude tude

Your name came off my lips like sandglass,
it sounded similar to the friend we impasse.

I always scared of the sunset,
but when we watched it go down
that fear would pass.
It wouldn't last.

The last time I saw us, it was through a spyglass.
I wonder if you really wanted my love
or if I finally broke the line by being an ass.
You told me we'd last.

I don't know what happened to you.
My world came crashing down into two.
I kept waiting for you.

I thought you'd keep your promise,
but you left me, *you*.
You left me in
super solitude.

> *tude tude*

I kept the pictures of our face,
from when we loved each other,
when everything felt so new.
Our time flew by
and I'm still getting out of
super solitude.

> *tude tude*

FIREWORKS

G.K.

Crying in front of the fireworks thinking of what we used to
be…
how you'd cuddle me.
Everything felt okay for once…
mental boundaries exploded.
I still wish there was you and me.

You came and left your spark,
blew up my heart,
left so many lesions…
the doctor had to cut the string.
Sometimes you visited me.
I heard your voice in the haunting darkness of my dreams.
Maybe your voice was the dream.
Maybe you never did visit me.
Maybe it was what could've saved me.

You broke my heart into smithereens.
Now, I rest in peace.
I think.

CITY I LOVE

G.K.

There's a city I love.
I'd love to live in.
There's a city I love.
Far and unreal.

There's a city I love.
One day this book will be sitting in it.
There's a city I love.
Far away from here.

I'm lost in the trenches.
Not knowing how to get there.
I can't leave all of this behind.
I can't be that far from here.

There's a city I love.
It's far from here.
There's a city I love.
I may never make it near.

DEPTH OF VISION

G.K.

Pushing back,

you can see what's really there.

When you're microscopic everything appears with a stare.

So, stop, just give it a glare.

Depth of vision is intense,

you can see far but really unclosed too;

you'll start being rude.

You'll want glue to fix it.

You'll want to be that thing you've always knew.

PARTY
G.K.

There's really nothing fun about this party.
Everyone that I see makes me sorry,
cause they had to see me too.

And if I had told somebody,
that I once loved a girl,
they'd laugh at me too.

They say that
"This party is great!"
Take a sip of alcohol,
never looking away.
I don't remember yesterday.

Being drunk in a parking lot,
trying to get back to me.
It's never easy
these days.

I think of all the pain.
All the trauma and things turn to gray.
I don't miss who I used to be.
I just miss how I used to be seen.

* * *

There's really nothing fun about this party.
Dear everyone that I see,
I'm sorry.
Hopefully now you'll love me too.

LANCE
G.K.

Well,
Lance was unique.
A man in the shop around the corner,
with a man he meets.

Lance and Jacob,
fair and cultured.
Another man glances at another's steal.

He questions what about them felt so surreal.
Was it the fact that they seem so perfect, and
love each other over Friday night beers?

Perhaps it is that.
Perhaps it is because they'll go.
The man will likely never see them again until,
Jacob is yours.

I KNOW

G.K.

I know that breathing too well.
I know that feeling too well.
I know that kind of heart break too.

Gleaming as trees past,
wondering what's best to ask.
When you try,
it's hard to see.
Just know I'll get you home.

Re-reading for scraps,
wondering if it's all real or not,
does that even matter?
Just know I'll get you home.

I know that breathing so much.
I hate the pain that feeling brings.
I hate that kind of heart break that never repairs.
I know it very well.

FINE WINE
G.K.

Nothing like a fine wine or two.
Sipping it, thinking about me and you.
Nothing about fine wine makes you think anything true;
it'll tell you who is who.

Wine so red it looked like the painful blood
when you left.
Wine glistening like the emotional eye
leaking teardrops wishing of death.

Here we are now,
I sit and rest, while you,
poke your new lovers with used needles
leaving them for dead.

They'll end up bruised,
each touch from another lover,
reminds the sharp pain of you.

There's really nothing like a fine wine or two.
Swallowing it, I stop thinking about you.

CRANNY
G.K.

Every nook and cranny, I want to fill with my heart.
I drove by your street, exciting for us to start.
You didn't know, but I'd stare at my phone waiting for the
text
"Have a good day."
It makes my heart bloom like a flower
the first day after it survives a fire.

Flying and finding,
who we're gonna be.
Splashing and slipping,
swallowing down a gyro.
I love every look you give me.

LOVE FILLED TEEN
G.K.

Swinging on a swing,
dancing on the floor,
ready any moment for someone to adore.
A love filled teen, excited.
Not knowing what to look for but
risks it all.
As they *slide*
on the
shades to be made.
> It's really brave.

Love filled teens,
never wary or afraid.
Looking for the pain,
they don't need.

It's why I stopped.
I want to be the love filled teen.
Giggles and never apart -
> I just have to fix what they tore apart.

TALL
G.K.

Tall but I managed to lose you in the crowd.
Tall but your height doesn't force a sound.
How can one be so ready for love,
yet so afraid?
How can one be so afraid of love,
still say yes to the smallest inch,
despite the derate.

Why does everything feel like a rebate?
When do I stop?
And after all this, they expect me to want it all?

FRESH PAGE

G.K.

A fresh page only stays warm for a moment.
It cools and ink dries.

A fresh page only stays fresh for a moment.
Then you rinse and repeat, awaiting the reaction.

A fresh page only stays unique for a moment.
Then it becomes the page before, left with no traction.

HOW DOES ONE

G.K.

How does one commit such an awful crime?
How could somebody kill someone else,
then feel nothing inside?
How could one ruin many lives.
An endless network of insufferable nights.
It's awful. Disgusting. Immediately revealing,
that that person has no fears.
How could one commit such an awful crime.
I feel awful seeing everyone cry.
How could one do this to another.
Is it worth it than leaving for the summer?

BOTTOM GRAIL
G.K.

Bottom grail,
holy.
Bracing with only.
How to share a moment so unique with anybody?
How to release so intently with somebody?

Granted afraid,
ignoring the risk,
forgetting the worth,
how does a grail remain?

It can't from a man who touched once.
It has to be thought to never be bailed,
never to be bought, never again on the rail.

Grails at the bottom, easily forgotten.
Maybe we're one,
maybe we should appreciate what we've gotten.

DROPPED ALONE

G.K.

Because of the others and how they treated me every single
day,
I've started to learn to keep my distance and never look away.
I am frail and afraid of being dropped alone.
It's a feeling to feel, one that comes multiple times a year,
a ship that can't turn back after it's seared.
Embracing each wave and droplet of water,
it could be the last.
What would even be the point of looking in the past?
When the ship sat on a dock, ready for sail.
Just to be thrown away and detached, they never cared.
Being dropped alone or dropped together is no fair,
the pain is too immense to see the pairs.

Lonely but stabilized,
yards of empty sea sweep,
what if you're not a fan of what's underneath?
Dropped alone the ship laid bailed.
Dropped alone the ship waits for mail.
It never comes.

Sitting lonely ready for another storm,
the ship begins to realize how unfit it is for there to be none.

Should it risk its life to be swept away?
Or does it just wait at sea and never be hailed?

WHY FOR WHY

G.K.

Why for why have it.
Why for whiny needs.
I thought you said you loved Whitney.

Oh-oh-oh

Why if your love is nude,
gentle and weak,
why have it if I get to have why for an answer?

Oh-oh-oh

Why do you run?
Why can't you do a simple wail?
Why do you stand there begging for the cheat sheet?

Oh-oh-oh

I gotta ask what you get from cruelty?
Is it the way my happiness fades for your
deadliest ego?
Or is it,
simple and malnourished like me?
The easiest factor is you don't need me.

Why for why?
Why for why?
Why for why?
Why'd you lie to me?
Why for why?
Why for why?
Why for why?

Why'd you have to realize you don't need me.

MISSED
G.K.

I miss love and what it becomes.
The smiles that cross two faces and a friend isn't one.
The vulnerability and intensity,
never wanting to say goodbye.
I miss the days where I saw that for me, myself and I.

Rather I mourn what I missed.
Rather I mourn what I never risked.

A gentle touch, sweeping eye.
Laugh after dark, way past midnight.
Sharing stories, some scary and rare.
Playing memories from Snapchat stories.

Some find this feeling not to be rare.
Not to be recognized as special,
or be cared.

I question if I'll find this feeling once again.
They say I will.
Who will it be with?
Why does it have to be so rare?

DIFFERENTLY

G.K.

What do I get for being seen so differently?
To be recognized as nothing,
never even me.

I could count and count, the time it has felt different,
never enough.
I could count and count, the stones that felt each touch,
more and more rough.

I may have to accept what will never be.
Equality and happiness,
peace for "all thee".

Maybe they slept well last night thinking of how tough they
made it.
Maybe they ate their nails this morning thinking of how
wrong I am.
Maybe they did nothing and never cared at all.
That's a thought, one that's hard to bear.

If me and my words aren't to matter,
why would my beauty or face,
my singing or writing,

if they just want me to say grace?

III
Discovery

CROSS FADE
G.K.

After the fade,
remains the dark.
After the dark,
remains a lark.
You can hear,
you can fear,
and you can feel,
either way you cannot
see anything near.

After the cross is the satisfaction.
After the cross comes the creek.
After the cross comes the hail.
How are you going to bare?

Once, you bit into a pear.
Out came the monsters,
ones you even thought were rare.
But now they were there.
None of it was ever fair.

TWITCHING FEATHERS
G.K.

The flowers twitch, moving left to right in an empty field.
It reminds me of the gift you never received.
Of purple endeavors,
an expression of simple needs.
Why not have the scraps of a twitching feather when that's
what you left me?

A dead bird, an eagle or owl for who?
The one who rang my doorbell when I was relaxing in my
room.
These feathers don't last until they get framed.
Or, until you take them back and bury them in place.

This feather can fold, it can break.
And it may, if it's truly the representation of "who's we?"

Carly waited at the river,
the stream going through her feet,
it's the most stability I've ever seen,
unfortunately.

Carly taught me good;
she also taught me bad.

She taught me to never smoke,
because addiction is bad.

I told her I didn't need smoke to be addicted,
she said, "No matter what, withdraw is always crooked."

BARELY STALE

G.K.

His glance,
lighting up the room,
everyone doesn't notice,
but he makes my eyes blur.

His jeans, slim and fit.
Perfect body image.
Stable as sand in an hourglass.

These are the things
that make me wanna prove,
straight to you,
I'm worth it and it'll work.
He's barely stale,
some would disagree,
they are not me.

I wish I was unique and special,
cool with that witty mood,
with a hair shake,
making me levitate.
I wish I was barely stale.

* * *

I'm sure you think about that for yourself.
To me you're barely stale.
No one else in the room makes me tear shit down including
all the nails.

You're barely stale.
Your eyes, a simple glare,
more than enough to quake my world.

Stare.

What do I say?
What do I do?
How can anybody be this rude?
How can you?
How can you, baby?

How do I move?
My friends make it a dare.
I do, everything I'm supposed too.

Pushing my way through the party crowd, trying not to lose
you.
Why wasn't anybody seeing you?
I wouldn't miss out, wouldn't miss my chance.
That's why I need you.

I tap on your shoulders, raise up a hand,
       introduced myself a little too bland.
  Your smile lights up a room, then, four words and I'm
doomed.
        I'm not like you.

              Oh.
            That's fair.

CALI
G.K.

California is my place to be.

So many artists have a song named after thee.

One time I listened to one, in a hospital room,
dreaming of making it out,
and making it there.

California is my place to be.

When I get there, fame will come to me.

Will it be unfortunate at times, absolutely.
Will it be fun in rare circumstances, absolutely.
Some reason, deep down inside me,
I feel that life is what I grew up made to need.
All of the hate, eyes and comments,
California is my place to be.

CROPPED

G.K.

There was never really anything like a cropped tee. I'd see it on sale and then I'd watch it leave.

I started to realize I wouldn't even fit the cropped tee and that thought started to bother me.

Shifting and swiftly, pushing down and away - my body was my greatest con I could tear.

I tried to tear, ripping parts out, leaving myself in a bigger hole then the one I had got.

Recovering and trying, gone and away, the cropped tee suddenly back in a flare.

Was told to buy it, by someone who couldn't know what or why, so the tee sat waiting for a life.

I pushed and severed the mental agony that became of me, trying not to hurt what I always see.

What I would do to be cropped like this tee.

Why can't being slim be for me?

They say you don't need it. Love who you are.

It's hard to love who I am with all of these scars.

Shifting and checking, night after night, I start to dig with the shovel - it doesn't put up a fight.

I dig and dig, finally striking gold, get praise and money from it - finally something I can hold.

It doesn't last. It doesn't save me a dime. It gets taken away by the wind as I climb.

I find myself stuck, gone and lost - my friends say "you're okay" but, I never believe them.

I try to crop, upwards, sideways and down.

The old me I had secured is buried and rare.

They say that cropped me wasn't the real me I should've wanted.

But I wanted it.

So, it be.

I tried and tried, cried and cried,

thinking I'm unlovable.

Why choose a penny over a dime?

Slightly trying to find what's fair, realizing it may never actually be there, what can I do?

Therapy comes and continues, dirt added on and on, and eventually we'll reach flat ground.

"But there's more dirt than before!" I explode before crying and going straight to the gutters.

"You'll be okay." I'm told. An epiphany of words I cannot feel, yet there's only three.

Why can I not believe what is told to me?

Why am I so broken and gone?

Maybe, it really is society after all. I'm tired of the string and thread.

The knot is here and dead.

I spent hours picking through it all, cutting loose the pieces that don't fit it at all.

I try to find what matters, what's really real.

What do I actually look like?

How do I feel?

Why is it that I can't like my body or who I am despite the reassurance?

Why am I this?

The formula, the system, has really failed us all - but what am I supposed to do after all?

The hole is getting more and more filled, bugs begin to crawl inside, adapting to my fall.

How do I stop this?

What am I actually supposed to do?

I want to dig it all out, shovel down.

I try, I dig, and I pull, dirt comes out but my arms don't feel.

I can't dig anymore physically.

Mentally, it's all I want to do, so I make a deal.

I use my strength to put the dirt back.

Letting there be a hill, and nothing flat, though it's not accepted and absolutely absurd.

I breathe in and out and call it a day.

I go inside and see what percentage I'm near.

When I awake, the brightest sun hits the room.

Sparkling in my closet is the tee that's more.

Except it isn't. It's no longer a tee.

It's a representation of pain and the horror I feel.

I try it on, feeling insecure and weakened, but maybe if I try more it'll feel more real.

I'm not sure if I can try. If I can make it real.

I haven't done it yet and I'm not nearby.

Full of fear, expecting the worse - the best is that the cropped tee is still a shirt I conceal.

NUDE
G.K.

Why nude?
What's so unique about the exposure of two?
I'm not sure why the secrets of one are one to fear.
The standards is the exposure is always wrong.
It's inappropriate and far too frowned upon.
Have you ever questioned if that was never real?
If a piece of clothing wasn't always used to conceal?
Sure, it sounds absurd, we are what we know.
What if we break the cycle and change for "the worst."

Why are the women only the ones shown nude?
Why cannot others be exposed and a sex appeal?
These questions are ones we avoid,
mostly because we are so adjusted to covering how we feel.

Nude feels so sacred, the word hard to utter outlaid.
What if you push yourself too, what becomes of you?
Do you become mystifying or simply unreal?
I hate to think of our world as it is.
One full of fear, one full of dread.

How can we push for change, when we're afraid of it?
How can we change a system, that's exposed for only one?

Where can we go?
What can we do?
What am I supposed to do if all I'm given is the grace from others that…
sometimes isn't even there.

Apparently, I haven't worked hard for what I have.
I was only given and never produced.
And sure, you could say I could never produce,
but that's me. I like men and it's not me being rude.

Apparently to some, I'm not enough of a minority to count as underprivileged.
I only mean what they see and how they perceive.
How am I supposed to be feel the self-relief of appreciation and love,
when I believe I am simply not enough.

Sometimes I do have to look near and far.
Sometimes I'm blindsided by who you really are.
Sometimes I have to realize that the protection and perfection I want isn't real.
Sometimes I have to accept that what I do is enough to be ideal.

I don't want to be ideal,

and reading this you could say you don't have too.
But if I did something unique,
you'd feel unnatural.

That's the reality of nude.
Women are "ideal" for it to many,
but what about what is not ideal?
Does it not matter and not funny?

I wish I could feel the sense of things feeling real.
Everything besides me feels extremely built and surreal.
I want to experience life as if I didn't know the lies.
I want to experience life as if I didn't see the exploitation.
But no matter, we cannot look away.
We have to question our morals and how it matters at the end
of the day.
Precise and extreme, that's what they want us to be.
Fuck it. Let me be me.

WHITE ROOM

G.K.

Sitting in a white room,
is where I am.
Not the kind of white room,
we always feared.

This white room has a view of the city,
four chairs,
and a table for studies.

Once upon a time, I visited a woman.
She sat and analyzed me,
wrote a study.

She said I was broken, but,
not too bad.
She registered me as an out-patient, but that's in the past.

Thinking back,
I know why I felt how I did.
I'm happy I'm better, though never cured.

Sitting in a white room,
is where I am.

Not the kind of white room,
that scared me so much, it ruined my friend.

PARADE

G.K.

You got the looks and
might see the parade.
I got the talent and
you'll think about it when it rains.

My heart was never weak,
it holds and strengthens.
Yours takes the brutal approach,
attempting to tear others to shreds.

MADDENING
G.K.

Isn't it maddening?
Filled with so much cheer?
Unaware of how much pain they've been spreading over the
years?
Anger is filled with so much direction,
maddening is filled with so much intention.

Isn't it maddening?
Seeing someone alone.
You might not be their type;
you can be their soul.

Isn't it maddening?
Frank.
A Vietnam vet,
now watches in regret.
He can't be what the kids are today.
He had to marry a wife,
who isn't here today.

Isn't it maddening?
Falling in love.
Breaking apart and losing your soul.

* * *

Isn't it maddening how we repeat?
How we lose our sense of gravity,
and…
repeat?

WHAT IF

G.K.

What if I decided it was time,

turned the car and didn't

snap out of it just in time?

Because of *you*.

Oh, *you*.

You haunted my dreams.

Haunted my past.

Took everything that,

I wanted to last

and ran away.

Never even thought of looking back.

What if *you* got the call,

it said I got shattered after all.

Would *you* feel any guilt?

Would *you* feel any pain?

Or would *you* avoid it like you did me,

when *you* saw the flame?

What if?

Oh, what if I changed my damn mind?
Went back in time,
made damage so deep,
you'd probably never keep in your mind.
Pain intolerance,
broken promises,
I'd died anyway when *you*
blinked and winked your eyes,
never said anything, let it take me by surprise,
goodbye.

NEVER
G.K.

I've never met a man who could

smile

like you…

I've never seen such innocence

swept away…

I've never seen a man who could

sit peacefully

like you…

Watching the world blur away.

I've never been pushed to act,

seen expectations pass,

So suddenly.

I've never seen a man just like you,

who was just like me,

but so much you…

I've never wanted to hug another,

hand on a stair rail,

like you…

Hair sailing in the afternoon.

FUNNY HOW YOU CARED

G.K.

You should be happy I took the time to find you,
found the way for us to talk.
We actually did it a lot.

You can take the excuse and leave the crime scene,
no one will stop you except the guilt in your dreams.
The ones you have of me.

It's funny how you cared,
you left so prepared.
It must've felt nice to take my compliments and boost the
drama between you
and your muse.
I heard you drank the next day till noon.

KID

G.K.

Am I the only one happy to no longer be a kid?

Maybe I'm in the sweet, middle spot where things can

be pretend.

Sometimes I feel bad for those in little school.

Unaware of what's to come, things they can presume.

Am I the only one happy to no longer be a kid?

Sometimes I miss the kid I was before the Edu.

I once cried, many tears from something I didn't know.

Turns out, I had an instinct, that I had grew.

Having to learn forced lessons.

I miss the noon nap time days with Legos to play.

BOOK STORE BOY
G.K.

I let you go bookstore boy.
We shared couple glances,
I was so scared of this white boy.
I don't know how I felt as you left.
Just the heartbeats I heard,
that stopped me from decoy.

I'll never see you again bookstore boy.
I was too scared and nervous.
Afraid of pain.
I'm sorry I didn't try.
I waved,
you waved.
You read a book,
bought one too.

Wish we could've shared a coffee,
or two.

FLY
G.K.

Ain't nothing like a guy.

Reminiscing, trying not to fly,

realizes I'm not a lie.

Then he flies,

back into my life.

Or at least he tries.

He never ever hit that same way.

He never ever came off badly.

I can deliver to any guy,

but no one accepts like you did, why?

Something about finding correction in correct.

Something about finding wastefulness in waste.

Ain't nothing like a guy.

Reminiscing, trying not to fly,

realizes I'm not a lie.

Then he flies,

and then he flies,

and then he flies,

so badly

badly

thought I wasn't what you need

you need

Flying, adolescent,

curly hair, black eyes,

luckily, I don't need a disguise.

You discount me as a lover,

could count the days till we were over.

And you want me back?

damn you that horny?

*that **you** need me?*

damn boy you crazy.

crazy.

I can't justify another touch; sometimes ask why

I feel so intelligent tonight.

Wondering if you'd actually take me back,

when i'm looking like that

* * *

I can't find the answer to what you need,

Why can't you tell me?

Shouldn't it be easy?

Maybe you're not the guy I thought you would be.

thought you'd be

ever wonder what i need

caught you thinking about the car seat

car seat

miraculous and stunning

broken away

send me a text and it'll be okay

kay

kay

kay

Ain't nothing like a guy.

Reminiscing, trying not to fly,

realizes I'm not a lie.

Then he flies,

back into my life.

Or at least he tries.

He never ever hit that same way.

Hopefully now he won't come off badly.

REMOVED WALLS

G.K.

When they remove the walls, I look like none.
One strange occurrence,
another drunk off rum.
Strangely, maybe I may fit in as one.
What if I don't see them as they see them?

I'm not sure why I feel so much dread.
A little moment, it felt awkward, emotions spread.
It's kind of abnormal they'd remove the walls that make me
look like none.
Now that it's gone, why do I want it back?

I'm not supposed too, yet I want too.
I dislike this exposure.
I hate this vulnerability.
I have to cope with it for a few moments,
I just want to run.

BROWNIE

G.K.

You want a brownie?

Want two?

cha-ching

Your bio says more,

than it should.

it's such a lie

Why is it that everyone matters to you,

but me?

but me?

I didn't do anything wrong,

fuck dating.

fuck
fuck
dating

SOMEDAYS

G.K.

Some days I have a happy end.

This was one.

Just one.

Sometimes I don't wanna get out of bed.

But today, I won.

I won.

My therapist says to take my meds.

When I do, it's got lens, makes me see clearly.

Clearly.

Generally, it is rare for days likes these,

with boring starts and awful evenings.

This was one.

Just one.

I thought I had an idea;

it was not.

Just a kick start.

I get news that may change things positively,
but there is another thing that stops me,
from being that level of happy.

I want coffee,
I want to write my book in bed.
I wanna be goofy,
I wanna laugh with my lover till I'm dead.

Isn't that funny?
Baby?

WAIT, I'M CONFUSED

G.K.

Wait, I'm confused.
You're telling me, WHO?
You went through all that for WHO?
My god.

Wait, stop, I'm confused.
What's going on here.
Did you lose?
Damn.

Wait, what the hell, I'm confused.
You're telling me it's like that now?
And stringing with that now?
Didn't see that coming.

Wait, give me a shot, I'm shocked.
How am I supposed to feel?
I'm feeling a lot.
Hope you don't get caught.

SEARED

G.K.

How did you do that?
How did you change the moment?
How did you manage to change it all,
and nothing at all?

I'm kept seared.
Mere seconds to dying of fear.
I wish I didn't know how this feels.

How did you get out of this so quick?
Climb the wall with your hands slick.
Mine can't even stick.

Uncertain of fate.
Certainly great.
What appears behind the gate?

G.K.

G.K.

Feeling really great.
Oftentimes I don't feel this great.
Sometimes it's even bait.
Sometimes I think I'm that bitch,
sometimes I think I'm okay,
sometimes I find the human experience in me,
then I overthink, and it fades.

Wondering drastically,
will my dreams come true?
They will I feel.
What will I become?
A game-changer.
How?
That is unknown.

It'll come when it comes.
It'll happen when it should.
I should trust the process and follow the bait;
might teach me a lesson and it'll help me be great.

Perfect isn't real and there is no right way in.
I'll look back in three decades, mid-success,

still wondering,
will my dreams come true?

THE THIRD LEVEL

G.K.

Nick sits at the third level.
Looking down he saw as the winds brushed against the tree's
green leaves.
There, the wind blows endlessly, existing negatively.
The wind blows everywhere.
The sky Nick see's is the sky we see.
His moon, our moon.
His sun, our sun.
Yet, Nick sits at the third level.

Very much up high.
Afraid, he sighs.
Looking down there's so much.
Dark ground,
guttered sidewalks,
yellow poles.
Nick sits at the third level.

Wind carrying something away,
dark grounds turned red,
guttered sidewalks flushing away,
and yellow poles painted,
Nick sat at the third level.

SLEEPING, WEEPING
G.K.

Have you ever had to move so intense?
Has your life ever come down to one single step?
Your foot was asleep.
All you could do was weep.

These moments are so newborn.
Everyone misses you when you're gone.
If only that step wasn't so far.

How to wake up and take that step?
How to take it back and remove regret?
How to get packed and leave on a plane,
than cross the country with human steps.

DECIDES

G.K.

Once in a while someone asks,
how my creativity gets *THAT* bad.
I think and think,
it feels like years,
then I say it decides itself.

Some days I may want something and another,
but no matter what it is and how,
it decides for itself.
Sometimes I feel my art is a person.
A person inside of me, trapped and left dying.

Why do I listen to what they may say?
They understand all of my pain.

YOU
G.K.

You loved my lyrics.
It's a shame you haven't read the heartbreak ones.

You loved my lyrics.
It's a shame you haven't read the new ones.

You loved my lyrics.
It's a shame you haven't read the ones after you.

I hope you feel shit you never have before.
I hope you love someone as much as I did you,
and then they shatter you.
Never show up to your most important moments
type of shatter.
My friends say that's petty of me, but,
honestly, fuck it.
It's how I feel, and you are why.

THE END
G.K.

Little more thoughts remain now.
Not much more left to say now.

Spread my word,
changed your view.
I'm scared.

What if after all this,
you realized I'm something to beware.

Will you look at me differently?
Never talk to me again?
Or is that my OCD speaking,
because this is the final page.

Little more thoughts remain now.
Not much more left to say… for now.

Within fall breeze
where yellow leaves fall,
      one leaves.

IV
Regulation

FELT THIS

G.K.

I haven't felt this alone since I met you,
and honestly, it's nice.
There's no drama, and,
I don't have to take as many pills at night.

I haven't felt the need to love like I did,
when I had met you.
I'm just working on my life,
recording journal entries on Tuesday nights.
I'm not dying.

I have a page almost everywhere.
My own small public figure.
Soon, I think it'll be big.
I'm also about to start another job selling iPhones.

Soon I'll get a new lover.
There'll be a picture of me kissing him on the cheek.
He'll be the one that will last forever.

Everything is still new to me.
I found out I was fighting an ace.
A never-ending race, and,

it would go till we're dying.

The leaves fall down.
The cars drive past.
Leaves my dress blowing in the gust.
My platforms making me taller than the last.
Things happen to be okay.
Everything is new to me.

Don't mind me.
I'm just walking down the downtown street.
Thinking about when things were sunny,
forgetting there were also clouds.

So, don't mind me.
I'm just looking around.
Watching as a couple tries on suits and gowns,
they're about to get married.
One look is so telling.

TREE TOWN
G.K.

I just wanna go to the tree town and,
not have to deal with other people,
forever.
I wanna go where the trees are always green,
the people aren't mean,
I won't have to be so hard on myself.
I just wanna go.
Just go.

Maybe someday I'll meet another,
he'd like to climb a tree with me,
get our own swing, and,
swing.
That's why I just wanna go to the tree town and,
not have to deal with other people,
forever.
However, I'm my own worst enemy, and leaving,
would be mean.

Maybe someday we'll have a kid,
and I won't wanna trap him in our tree house,
so we'd leave.
I just wanna be at peace.

I am so marginally bad.

Everyone is mad at me right now, kind of bad.

I don't know how to control this, kind of bad.

What I did upset my family, kind of bad.

I write to cope.

I type to cope.

They see it as me being ignorant and selfish.

It wasn't my fault for the explosion.

Maybe I should've stayed home.

Why am I so marginally bad?

WOULD

G.K.

I would like to not talk about you.
Not think of you.
Sometimes, I just have too because,
the thought of you ruins a moment.

Happiness comes with a dream.
A dream to love you again.
What do you dream?
Is there ever one of me?

HIGH LOVE
G.K.

Looking back one thought always stayed with me,
did you need to be high to love me?
Each moment and date, never could keep a puff away.
At least you were trying.

I hadn't smoked then,
I do now,
likely not as much as you, but,
the idea of doing it with you died with a frown.

I still just wonder however,
did you need to be high to love me?
Is that what it takes to love me?

EXPOSURE

G.K.

I learned exposure is the best teacher, so,
I go to the theater,
to heal from what we had.
It's always really sad.

It's okay though,
I've learned to deal.
I've learned to accept
what's not even here.
I've learned to heal.

Working hard,
dedicating my life to helping another,
broken and scarred from another like you.
I'd be his friend.
He's strong.

OLD
G.K.

As we get older, we forget more of each other, yet,
we still do the exact same things.
Exact things, sometimes too close to each other.
Sometimes too close we see each other doing them.

Your bones growing and resting in place,
my mind traveling lightning fast,
each day another departed and changed,
and it has to be okay.

This is a hard night.
This is the night I just wish you'd call.
I don't want to cry and miss anymore.
I've done it too long.
Teardrops falling onto my keyboard.
Each letter tap, a puddle splash.
Will things ever be okay?

I know that there are others,
it's just you're all I've ever known.
That's why I just can't move on.
The idea and sense of love is only you.
That's the only love that made it to love.

* * *

These days we live down the street from each other.
You don't know it though.
I think about it every time I drive to a store though.
I could've been there for you all year though.
Just help me.
I'm not that strong.
My bones are weak and unsettled.
Frail, and you're the hail heading right for it.
Just come to me.

These days, you think I fully moved on and hate you.
Fun fact, I think of that about you too.
It doesn't make it easier,
just half as bad.
I can't be the one to reach out.
That's on you.
I'm just waiting for you.
Tirelessly, as we get older.

I was supposed to be done with this now.
How could I?
It's my biggest open wound.
I think it's okay to still feel all this hurt.
It probably makes me look bad these days to you.
I guess it is what it is.

Maybe one day I'll learn how to fully forget and lose the spec of love left.

Maybe I'll learn that as we get older.

DREADED FIGURES

G.K.

and when I broke her heart, I responded right back to her.
"Please, I didn't want this to be me. I didn't want to go to war.
I'd rather be a thief."

The men around him laugh, gentle holding their flasks.
They drink a sip, because they've gotta make it all last.

I never wanted war,
never would've left home,
kept my mother at home crying.
My brother just died,
and my mother's gonna find out I'm next when
sarge pulls up the drive.

The men around him cheer, gleefully digging their grave.
The consequence of an action little tales tell but are never fair.

I wish I could tell her,
that I miss her.
I wish I could tell her that I wanna make eggs,
repay her for all the bread she once fed me with.
I wish I could tell her.

* * *

The men lower their head. Eyes full of sorrow.
They know what's next, an awful tragedy for a ménage.
And they head to sleep, prepare for the next day.
The soldier spoke his truth, a soldier carried his body the
whole way back.
He heard his story, a message to send to a mother who
couldn't hear back.

After the war, this soldier found his way to the home.
He knocked on the door and a frail lady appeared when it was
opened more.
He said
I wish I could tell her,
that I miss her.
I wish I could tell her that I wanna make eggs,
repay her for all the bread she once fed me with.
I wish I could tell her.

The mother cried.
Mourned her two sons, but
the message finally arrived.

HASSEL

G.K.

A hassle and bad is what you were,
like the camera they used on the moon.
You were red and met green
when I was blue.

Black is the color of ink I used
to write tens of pages about you, but,
now I sit and enjoy my iced coffee as best I can.

Silky and shiny,
unique and new,
I'm feeling something,
getting new fuel.

Reminiscent and nostalgic,
memorable as the smell of the ET theme park ride,
I've started to learn how to not think of you as best I can.

Before, my darkest nights were when my thoughts of you had
too much spotlight.
Now, my darkest nights are when I catch a slight thought of
you.
I guess I made it through.

Pushed through the limits, past the max.
Roaring away.
I still often wish you cared.

SPICY HOT

G.K.

I ain't ever felt this hot, so
spicy,
spicy,
hot.

Pull up in the lot.
Guess what they got?
They got that big one for me baby.
That glide and stride baby.
You gonna need the pope to fix me baby,
cause I'm so hot, so
spicy,
spicy,
hot.
God damn.
I'm being a lot but,

ring ring
gotta call for a cab.
another *fling fling,*
I'm constantly had.
They want me cause I'm

hot, so
spicy,

spicy,
hot.
So hot I had to call the cops.
They left me with them dirty ass socks.
No deal.
It kept happening cause my stories got hot, so
spicy,
spicy,
hot.
Someone wanted attention so they dropped off
dirty,
dirty,
socks
at my front door.
True story.

FREE SUMMER
G.K.

I got
a summer bucket list and there's a lot, yet
it's only June.
I've got the time of day.

Ain't nobody comes as a surprise,
I've let the hopes just die,
it's alright.
I'm living a drama free summer.
Drama free summer

Yea I think about you,
it might suck for a day or two,
then I move on and shoot more film,
madly.

There isn't an app,
causing the absurd and creeps to act the way they do,
I've been vibing and thriving,
living a drama free summer.
Drama free summer

All my friends are out of town,

it's alright because I'm around,
laying in my bed,
planning my next project
or two daily,
living a drama free summer.
Drama free summer

Eating shaved ice next to geese,
having fun, ends meet,
continuing to have another day.
Hanging with Toby,
not thinking about you daily.
Everyone's getting corny,
posting videos with their boys,
their boys with no respect to girls,
you can almost taste the bitterness from the void.

Drama free summer,
no bummer,
summer of love,
summer of me,
can feel the heat above.
Being frank,
I rewatched Mank,
it was really fate.
Drama free summer.

Chewing gum forever.
Drama free summer.
Feeling numb-er.

RAN INTO
G.K.

Run into the season of fun and
never lose yourself.
Run into love you have,
between you or anyone.
There's no darkness with some light,
just make sure you open your eyes and
run into the season of fun,
never, ever look back.

There's love in everyday,
just trust yourself and you maybe will
discover what it means to have fun
in a summer where nothing is done.

Run into the summer of fun,
and never lose yourself.
Run into the friend you can make,
never forget their soul.
Remember every day.
Remember everything.
Run into the season of sun.
Never lose yourself.

* * *

Never give up on yourself.

Never fail by making your heart melt.

Just run into the summer of sun.

Just run into the season of fun.

Never lose yourself.

The reason we want a new reality is because we cannot cope with living now.

REFRACTION

G.K.

Your refraction killed,
glass shattered all on the floor.
I was blinded to the core.
Now I've picked up the pieces,
made them more.

Your refraction had a sharp edge,
unsupported ad unsupervised,
you cut me and left that one scar.
Now it's fading, even more after the fall.

Your refraction,
an image of your reaction,
you lost all your passion,
I got more too.
Your refraction,
now used for the mirror ball that
I sing and dance next too.

LIGHT STAINS

G.K.

Light stains leaving trails till afternoon.
Effortless, broken, torn from the view.
Eye drops held back, branch in a fire.
Light stains above, afternoon showers.

Supercharged motion,
waiting for the company,
can't help but feel I'm only bad.

Though it's not true,
good I may do,
that all goes away with one mistake I made.

I tried,
I suffered,
I'm too average at the end of the hour.
What a screw up I am,
a rotting flower.

CRACKED ROAD
G.K.

A cracked road within the shadows of a car, two
patients waiting for an ambulance except,
they never called.

Times moved and clouds passed by
two patients became two standbys.
As others drive past, headlights move in a flare,
they can only think about "what if they cared?"

Once, they had felt care,
thought with no drought.
Once, they felt okay,
carried every hour.

Now they can no longer be any which where.
Fair isn't real, it doesn't care enough to heal.
Daring and sharing, bearing aware.
Pain intolerance, insufferable at most,
two standbys wait for an ambulance to come.

They've never had this accident besides this one.
It's one of their faults for not caring for it all.
They don't know everything.

They don't know one.
They hate being the thoughtless ones.
Here they are.

The cracked road gets filled with oil.
It leaks and catches flames,
the car begins to boil.
A gas tank explosion,
hopelessness aware,
they lose their life,
is that fair?

BOYS AND THEM
G.K.

Boys and them are so hot.
Swiftly, fluffy hair.
A filled smile, edge to edge.
Eye perfection, eye adoring.
I wanna fuck around with one right one.
Twirl together under the gleaming, reflective sun.

Their names gentle,
mostly with no scruff,
I want to be a part of what they become.
Though they're mostly not gay like me,
it's nice to give a glance and stare.

A kiss on the lips can do so much,
fill a heart,
or leave a hole bunched.

Something about men don't do what the girls can.
I just don't feel the lust or grand romance.
Friends to more friends,
me and girls will be.
Love to more love,
me and boys can ever be.

GRAND HEADROOM
G.K.

Laying in the bed after the dare,
felt you up,
in the bathroom you are now.
Logan with the sharp "L" jawline,
fabricated, but cared.
This is simply just a reminder,
we had so much grand headroom.

Pushed against the drawing board,
headroom left in the backroom,
it became all about me and you.
Finders keepers,
I'm the weeper.

Delicate and deceiving,
broke but healing,
gentle by the light of a hue,
clap and it fades,
we can do this every day.

Logan with the great logic,
hair fairly wary,
laying on your pillow,

staring.

GLITTER COUCH

G.K.

Super rail, emotions constantly flying higher.
Gripped down, hammer found.
Pair simple and lower, house floor four goer.
Glitter couch moving moreover,
old party balloons dying, getting lower.

Lock lip stuck, arched against the armrest,
this glitter gonna last forever.
Moreover, there's nothing slower,
than the building temptation to take things a step further.

Nothing funny, if there was, it would be over.
People left and now he's a show-built showoff.
Trickling surprises all over, where will he go till we're over?

Super rest, arched back.
What we knew went, cranberry from Italy bent.
Hover, we start feeling like we're flying over the top.
Vocal grasp, cupped glass.
Everything shatters after the fall of the nightstand.

VISTA CRACK
G.K.

Vista crack revealing more,
more and more over,
those two just keep getting slower and slower.

This crack growing older,
people in view bounce,
they're starting to finally get found.
This vista crack finding its way.

Got a view of each hair from the vale,
watch as those tree branches blow slower.
Looking left to the right,
full perspective in the vista crack,
it snapped.

It snapped farther than the getaway trap,
funny how they get discovered just when they learned to
adapt.
Everything keeps getting unwrapped with the vista crack.

Police pulling up with their wiretaps,
they're ready, black-capped.
This vista crack about to pull a war out of its concrete blocks,

unfortunately, they're all trapped.

FOLK LOAD

G.K.

I got a folk load,
it's a little lot.
Everyone knows what happened when we fought,
it blew up in your face,
you wanted to run away that day.

Everybody now wants to know what you got,
finding ways to keep that secret sacred,
or maybe not.

They showed me my down to the fountain,
water always new, there's always something brewing,
or not.

Saw you dancing crossing the lot with her.

When we passed the crossroad, it had exploded.
Everybody went to get a piece of the road,
it eroded.

Got the view of a dime in the water, baby.
It was a lot.
It was all I got.

ANNA
G.K.

Anna's the worst,
got her hands grasped around my throat,
pushing more down than they did when they told me to rot.

Anna ain't got a lot,
her little control speaks so much and it's hard to forget.
Feeling weak, deep down.
Feeling off, put into the category of hot.
Anna ain't got all that,
she does over me.

I ain't ever heard a voice sound so deep,
on repeat,
so fluently.

She's getting caught, burned on the bridge,
accidentally turned her thoughts and fought.
I thought she was dead, she was not.

Anna keeps going, she ain't ever leaving us alone.
What am I supposed to do to get her away?
I've spent so much money on things she bought.

COME ON, COME ON

G.K.

Come on, come on!

Hurry before they burn our place.

Take our sacrifice and use it against us.

Turn the pitchforks from themselves and onto the ones who tried.

We better turn and dash - grasp for each last second we can.

Come on, come on!

Come on silently.

We don't want a whisper.

The more we fear, the more we can hide.

There are ways we can find our new lair.

Come on, come on!

They're on their way to burn our face.

They are approaching, feeling our adrenaline in the shape of a thought.

Relentless! Unbounded.

Where are we silent?

Come on, come on!

I can tell you this story anytime but now.

We have to live to thrive.

We have to fight instead of die.
We can do this if we try.

Come on, come on!
Don't let the flames smoke you out.
Escape from the rage left inside.
Run from the deepest depths.

Come on, come on!
Let's make them run.

MOUNTAIN WOODS

G.K.

How the mountain woods push and thrive.
The animals enjoying every feast.
The creeks finding their perfect flow,
ants slamming their feet on the ground.

There are mountain woods,
where we run and hide,
and stay alive.

How the trees run from the open fires.
The deer's dash from the wolf in the bush.
The owls fly high, land on a branch.
The flowers growing and growing,
effortlessly.

There are mountain woods,
where we run and hide,
and stay alive.

How the rocks hold themselves in gravity.
The little snowflakes giving water from the drought.
The answer of a bird's call,
waiting birth from the eggs.

* * *

There are mountain woods,
where we run and hide,
and stay alive.

The woods grow far and deep,
fires less likely.
Seen to be less.
Hour is an hour.
Day and night, the only time.

These are the mountain woods,
where we run and hide,
to stay alive.

THERE AIN'T
G.K.

There ain't a word,
there ain't a speech,
I know you got a question, but I cannot eat.

I took the step,
followed the recipe,
it all turned out broken in my sleep.

There ain't many words to say to you, there
ain't a speech to speak,
all I know is I got you and you got me.

There ain't the chance,
I can up and leave,
I know that you could gleefully.

I pick up rags,
wipe up the blood from the dream.
There ain't an answer to speak.

DRIVING SAND

G.K.

Sand flying back,
landing in their eyes,
their ears,
maybe they shouldn't have looked at me.

I was driving in the sand,
sand in the treads of the tires.
I was drifting in the goodbye,
and a different hello that comes after.

Sand flying back,
lands right into the ocean floor,
wet and gripped,
I left with speed.

I was driving in the sand,
the fear of a band of stares.
I was drifting so they'd miss my eyes,
by doing so,
they also missed the look of goodbye.

ROOFTOP

G.K.

On the rooftop,
yellow hoodie covered the white tee.
We're in a parking lot, overviewing the city.
A perfect analog photograph, taken on Gold.
An exciting and unforgettable evening away from the cold.
You somehow forgot.

You somehow forgot how free it was,
how effortlessly I took you,
how changing it truly was.

I had bought those tickets for someone else.
Someone who decided I wasn't enough, so,
I took you instead.
Yet, you treated me the same, as they once had.
I let all the things you said disappear, God bless I say one bad
thing.
Of course, I didn't mean it.
It was a mistake that I made.
Was it worth it to end all the fun we had made?
Kendall?

TOBY
G.K.

When I met you, we were both down.
In different places, yet in the same town.
I tried to feed you, you just explored.
It was all as new to you as it was me.
I took you home and we made each other so much more.
My little dear, my biggest and best friend,
the one that will never judge me,
I can always say I love you, big baby.

Whenever I see you, I fall all over again.
You get excited and wag your tail.
You jump, kiss and have that sparkling bark.
I love you Toby, you're my emotional support.

You were there after the relapse.
There when I needed you there.
Cared when I needed you to care.
Asked for my love because I am always willing with you.
I love you Toby, my emotional support.

They said it would be hard, impossible,
for a broken boy like me to have an amazing boy like you.
Yet here we are.

Through light and dark, I'll be with you to the end.
I will always love you and your little tooth,
your sharp brown eyes and flashy tongue.
I will always love you Toby, my emotional support.

NORMAL END

G.K.

I'm okay.
I drift and live.
I make projects all on my own.

I work fairly hard, but
blame myself
into thinking I'm cold.

I've realized over these years,
that I may feel so much pain, but
I'll always get out of jail.

The end is technically supposed to be grand,
for you to wish there was another page.
Sometimes the best endings,
are the ones left to fate.

End Note

It's often hard to find ways to present the healing process. It is different for everyone. I still suffer with it and have my good and bad days and likely will until the next one stays.

If anything, I hope this collection gave you a feeling of normalcy, security and also a taste of what extreme vulnerability can look like from my end. I am very scared that this book will come off in a way I didn't mean. Perhaps that is because the projects I had completed prior to this year (and quarantine) were judged under a microscope.

The main reason I ended up releasing this collection of journaling, songwriting and poetry is because... I can. I like to have something I can hold and showcase. Something I can own. Something you can own. Something that can sit on your bookshelf (hopefully), and you could pick up and read.

I've learned that when I make something that I am proud of and become worried of the response, I should simply not look at it. A skill I learned from every single lovely YouTube comment I received in my youth. I also learned that pictures can be as harmful as words. They can capture a single moment in which the world just stops. Sometimes, I would like to live in that paused frame. I'd sit down on an empty table and think about why I got what I got and why what was taken was taken. I likely wouldn't even get an answer to those questions. What would you ask yourself?

Now, I spend my time working hard in therapy weekly. I work on personal projects most days of the week (like this one was). I work hard at school, and I also cuddle, pet and hangout with my best baby, Toby. A lot. He's perfect. I've closed myself off from love mostly because I don't want what happened to me to happen again. It will. Maybe that will be the topic of the next book I make. Maybe, I'm already working on my next book.

This book has gone through a lot of phases over the last few months. I wasn't actually sure when it was going to end. I kept spiraling. I kept thinking and drowning. The difference from then to now is that... I want to be done putting words in this project. Yes, that does mean that another new project will be opened as soon as I export this one. No, it doesn't mean that project is the one you will receive from me. Or maybe, just maybe, you might get it. I'm sure it will have a lot less to do with love. Hopefully, it'll be a subject more mature and thought provoking.

The pages you read are very meaningful to me. It captures the wrong I've been dealt from so many different people and the way I also did so many things wrong. It captures the little characters in my brain that live in a fantasy world. It captures the issues of my mind and how I cope with them.

To people written about in this book that are reading these pages, hello! I chose my words in a certain way that gives the upper layer without exposing what my mind truly says now. A lot of the pages were written in a time when blood still dripped.

Now, I still have the scar.

G.K.

Gabe Kanae was born in Reno, Nevada in 2003. He started making content at the age of eight by recording himself play video games on his television screen. Today, at the age of nineteen, Gabe has achieved over ten million views on internet videos, is a full-time college student, works as the opinion editor for the college newspaper and is now a self-published author and poet.